Tiny

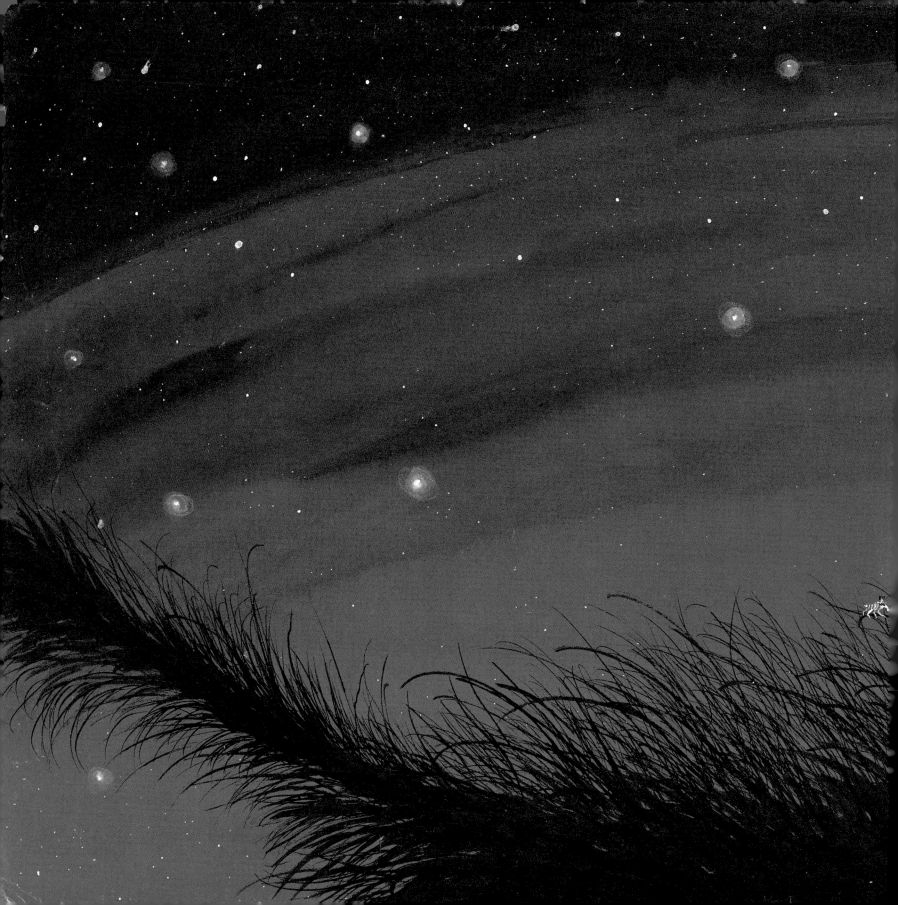

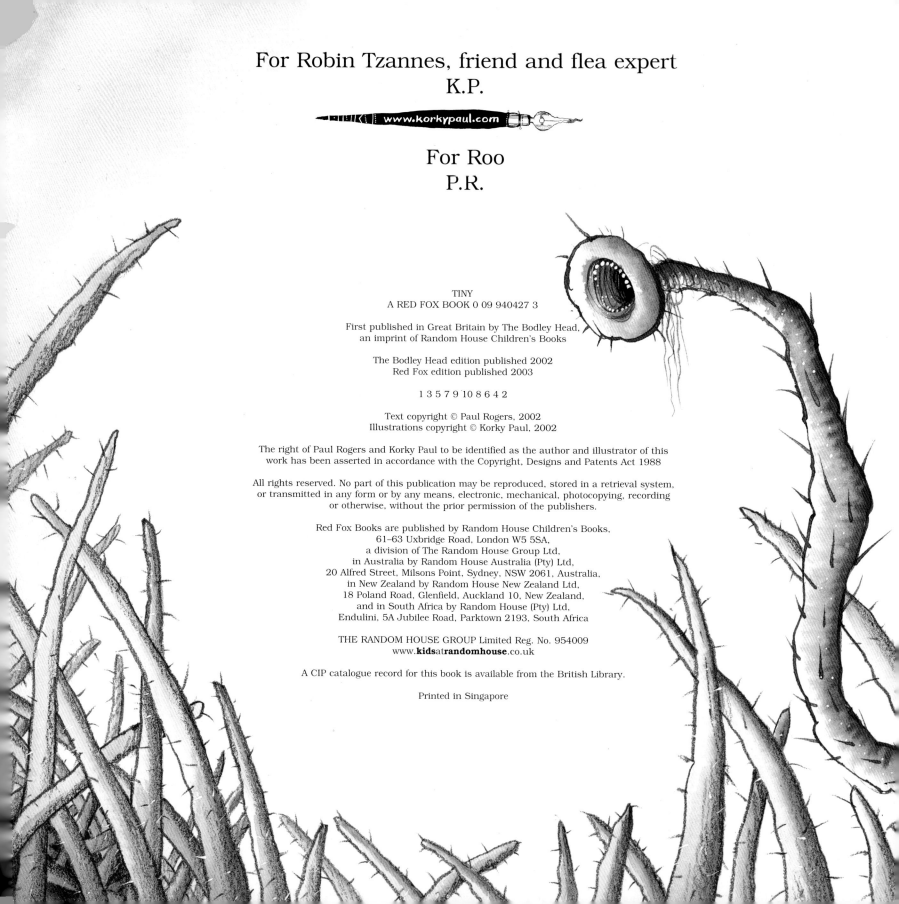

For Robin Tzannes, friend and flea expert
K.P.

www.korkypaul.com

For Roo
P.R.

TINY
A RED FOX BOOK 0 09 940427 3

First published in Great Britain by The Bodley Head,
an imprint of Random House Children's Books

The Bodley Head edition published 2002
Red Fox edition published 2003

1 3 5 7 9 10 8 6 4 2

Text copyright © Paul Rogers, 2002
Illustrations copyright © Korky Paul, 2002

The right of Paul Rogers and Korky Paul to be identified as the author and illustrator of this
work has been asserted in accordance with the Copyright, Designs and Patents Act 1988

Red Fox Books are published by Random House Children's Books,
61–63 Uxbridge Road, London W5 5SA,
a division of The Random House Group Ltd,
in Australia by Random House Australia (Pty) Ltd,
20 Alfred Street, Milsons Point, Sydney, NSW 2061, Australia,
in New Zealand by Random House New Zealand Ltd,
18 Poland Road, Glenfield, Auckland 10, New Zealand,
and in South Africa by Random House (Pty) Ltd,
Endulini, 5A Jubilee Road, Parktown 2193, South Africa

THE RANDOM HOUSE GROUP Limited Reg. No. 954009
www.kidsatrandomhouse.co.uk

A CIP catalogue record for this book is available from the British Library.

Printed in Singapore

Paul Rogers & Korky Paul

Tiny

RED FOX

Once upon a time there was a flea called Tiny.

And the flea lived on a dog

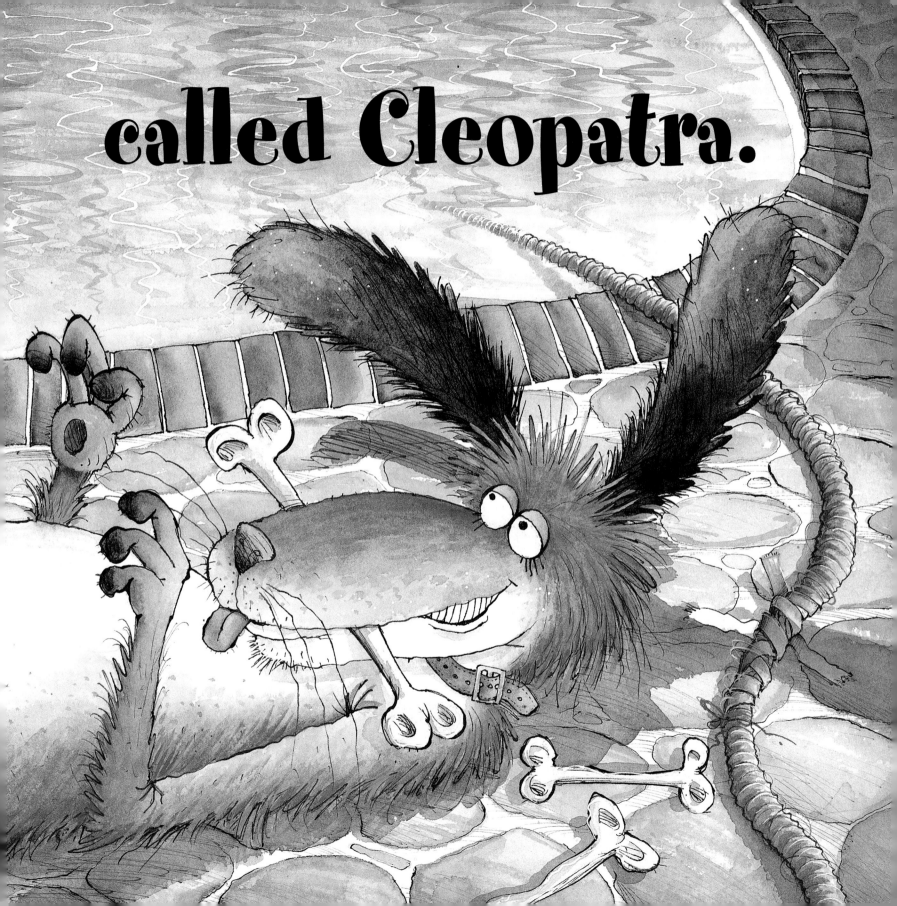

called Cleopatra.

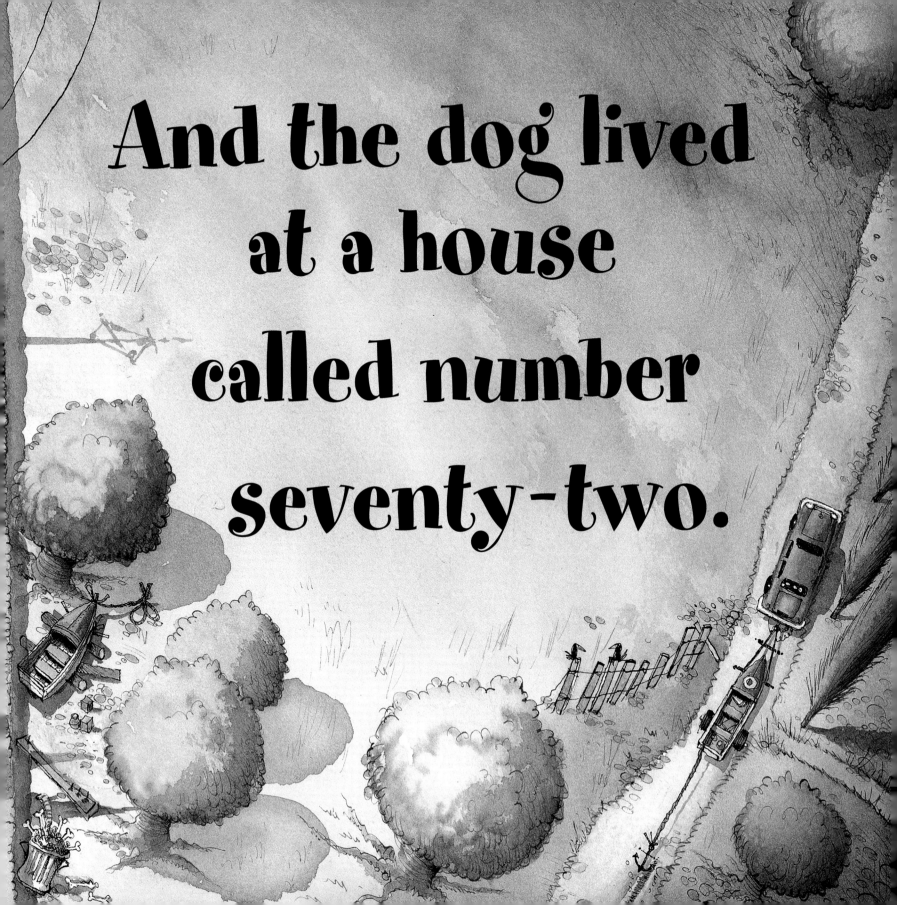

And the dog lived
at a house
called number
seventy-two.

And the house was in a road

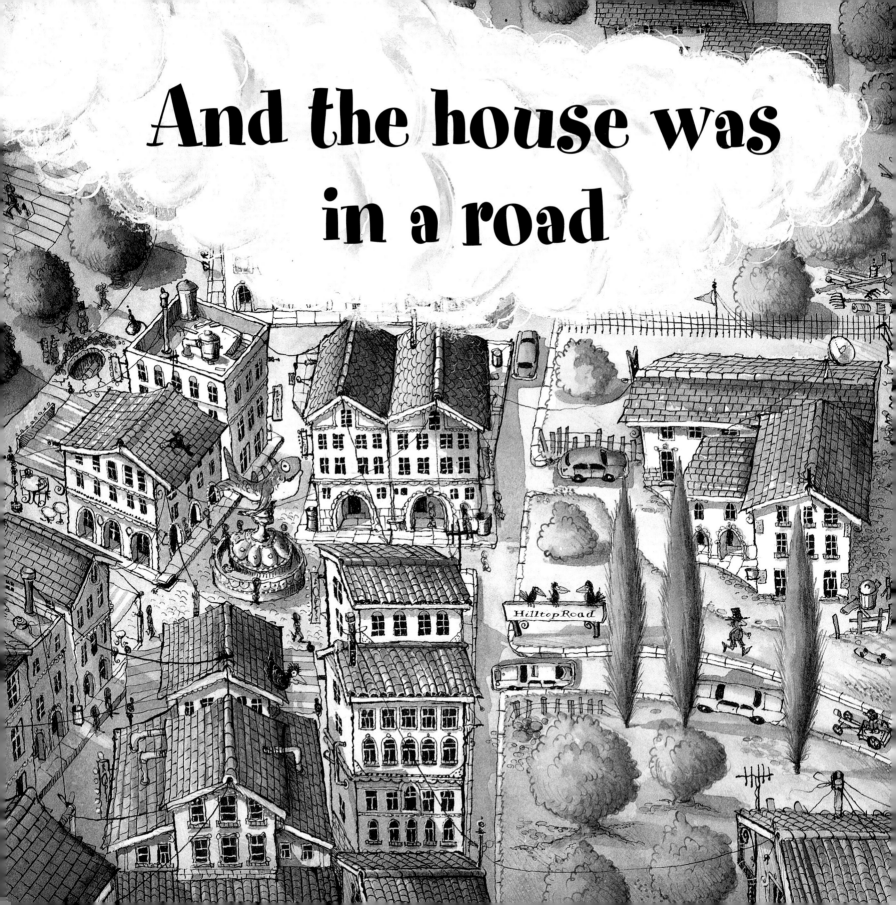

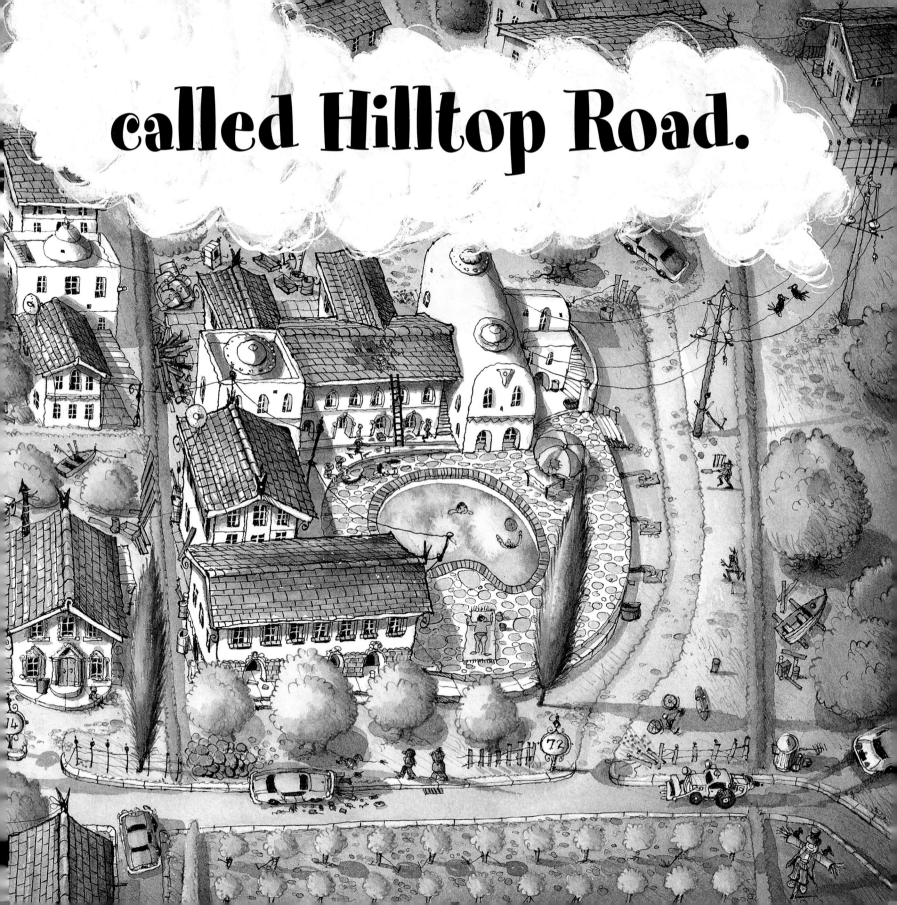

called Hilltop Road.

And the road was in a town

called Remembrance.

And the town was on an island

called Great Hope.

And the island was in the ocean on a planet

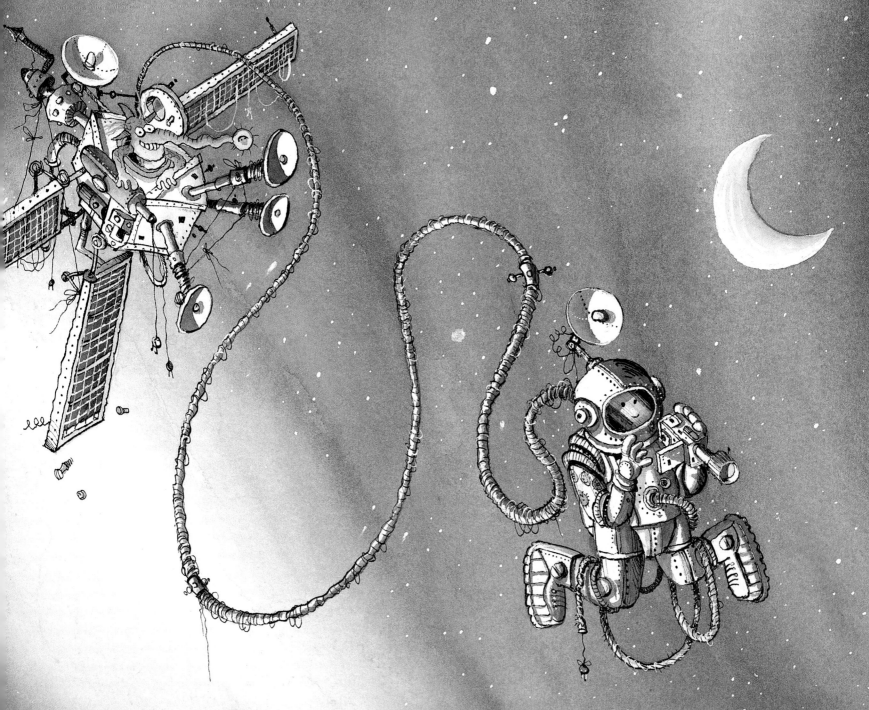

called Earth.

And the Earth was in a sort of heavenly merry-go-round

full of huge stars far bigger than the sun.

And one evening Cleopatra had a jolly good scratch and
Tiny fell off and landed on his back.

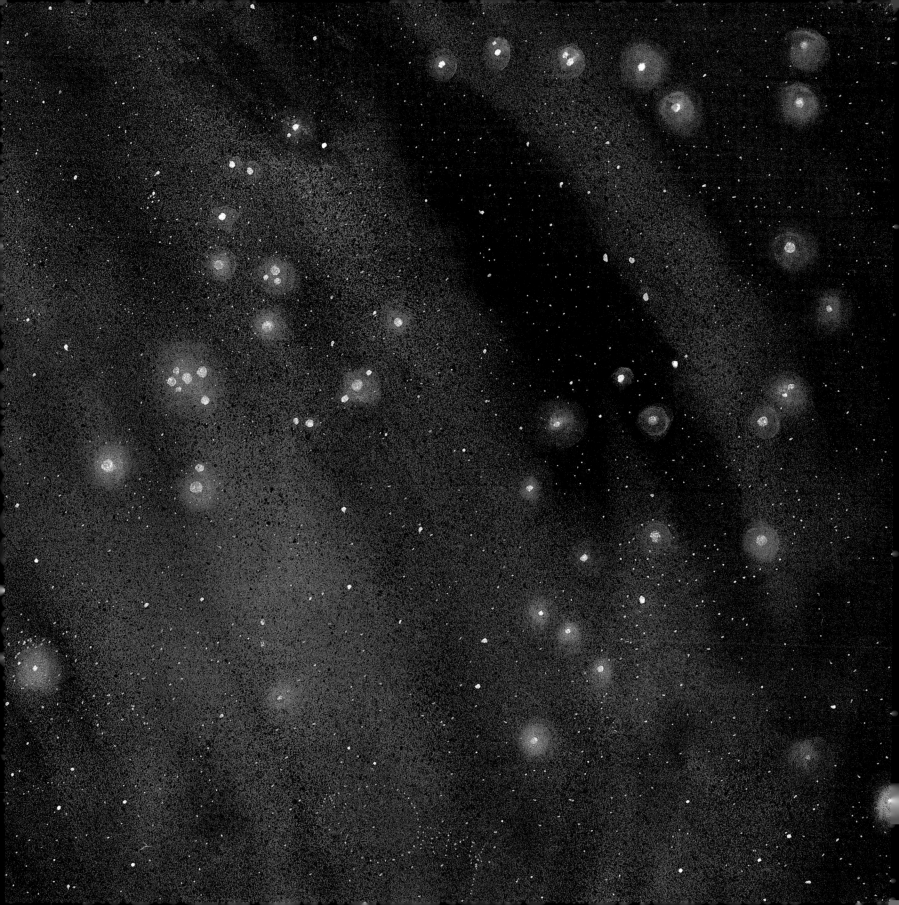

"Perhaps it doesn't matter that I'm so small after all."

And thinking that happy thought, he sat there waiting...

...until the next dog came along.

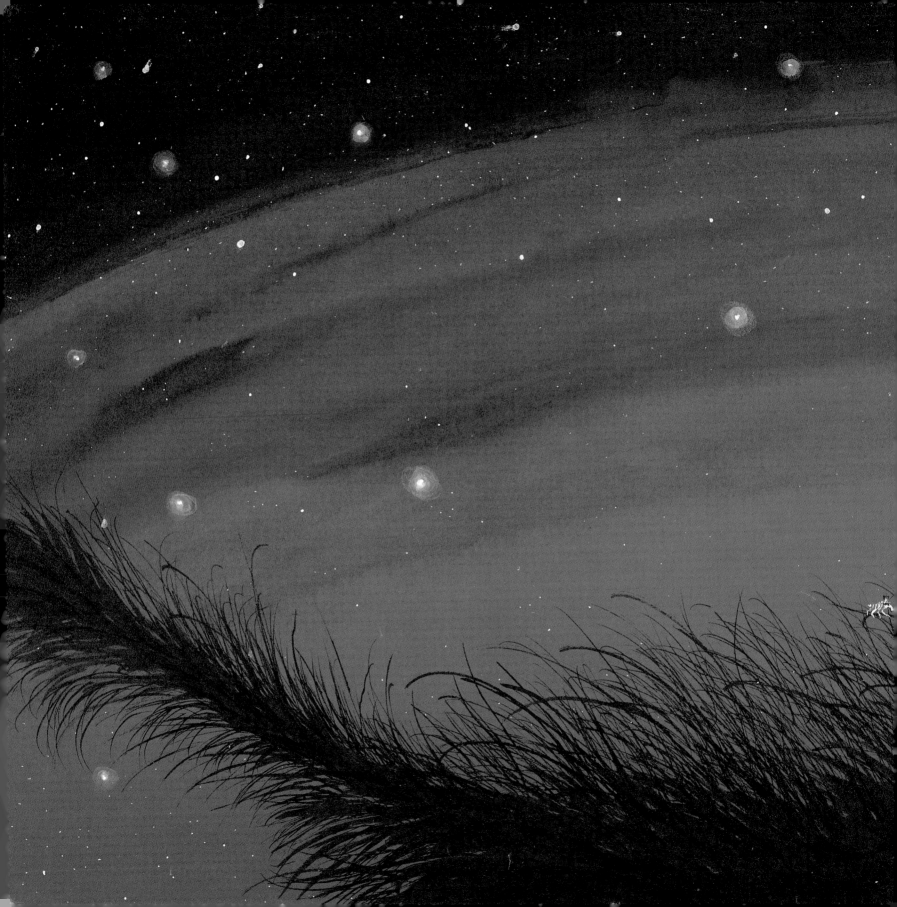

Other books you might enjoy:

The Dog That Dug by Jonathan Long and Korky Paul

The Cat That Scratched by Jonathan Long and Korky Paul

The Duck That Had No Luck by Jonathan Long and Korky Paul

The Wonky Donkey by Jonathan Long and Korky Paul

Froggy Plays Football by Jonathan London and Frank Remkiewicz

Friends Together by Rob Lewis